This book, and my garden, would not exist without the friendship
and good example of Thisbe Nissen. —L.S.

For Lucious. This book could not have happened without your support,
encouragement, and comic relief. —S.C.

Author's Note

The Forever Garden is based very loosely on a Talmudic story:

Honi is walking down a road and chances upon a man planting carob
seeds. Honi asks the man whether he plans to live another seventy years so
that he might harvest the fruit of this tree. The man explains to Honi, "I was
born into a world with carob trees. Just as my ancestors planted for me,
so I plant for my descendants."

"*L'dor vador,*" we say in Hebrew. "From generation to generation." This is
how traditions survive through the ages, how the world continues to grow.

For me, the magic of the story is (of course) in the idea that we should all
tend the earth and care for our descendants. But I also love the idea that in the
very teaching of this story, the man has educated Honi, has planted another
kind of seed. I love the idea that people are gardens too, and that they bear the
fruit tended by many generations of gardeners.

There is also something particularly lovely about the relationship a child
can have with a neighbor. In *The Forever Garden,* I hoped to explore that
relationship—of a child watching, living beside someone, learning from that
person, even though he or she may eventually go away. For me, the idea of
gardening is such an apt metaphor for friendship. We put in the time and effort
because it is worthwhile to do so, not because of what we expect to harvest.

In a sense, we are each a Forever Garden.

Text copyright © 2017 by Laurel Snyder • Jacket art and interior illustrations copyright © 2017 by Samantha Cotterill • All rights reserved.
Published in the United States by Schwartz & Wade Books, an imprint of Random House Children's Books, a division of Penguin Random House
LLC, New York. • Schwartz & Wade Books and the colophon are trademarks of Penguin Random House LLC. • Library of Congress Cataloging-in-
Publication Data is available upon request. • ISBN 978-0-553-51273-1 (hc) — ISBN 978-0-553-51274-8 (lib. bdg.) — ISBN 978-0-553-51275-5 (ebook)

The illustrations in this book were rendered in pen-and-ink on watercolor paper and colored digitally.

MANUFACTURED IN CHINA
2 4 6 8 10 9 7 5 3 1
First Edition

the forever garden

Laurel Snyder &
Samantha Cotterill

schwartz **&** wade books • new york

In sunshine and shower, in darkness and wind,

Honey tends her garden....

Honey's knees are always muddy.

Sometimes, when it's cold outside, she tucks her garden in.

Shhhh . . .

When the lettuces are small
and new, Honey thins them.
Her scissors say *shnick!*

And the peas climb up.

Honey pulls her beets from
the ground with a shout that
scares the chickens.

"Ha!"

Honey sings to the kale.

She says it sings back, but I can't hear it.

Not even when I listen close.

I hang on the fence in the mornings.

Honey feeds me tiny carrots washed under the pump.

Yellow tomatoes the size of marbles. They taste like sunshine.

When it rains, I watch from the window.

Sometimes Mom sends me to Honey for an egg to bake with.

Honey's eggs are pink and green. Smooth and speckled.

The chickens get mad. They scatter. *Cluck!*

"Presto!" says Honey as she slips an egg into my hand.

The egg is warm.

Each Friday night, I ask Honey to dinner.

She brings bouquets of funny things.

Squash blossoms,

rosemary,

raspberries on a prickle branch.

Nothing matches, but everything fits.

And the table smells like a meadow.

On nice nights, Honey eats in her garden.

Beans and salad. A jug of water from the pump, tinkling cold.

When the fireflies come out, I go over for dessert.

Honey *always* has a cookie.

I have two.

Or three.

But one day . . . there's a sign in Honey's yard.

Angry letters shout: **FOR SALE!**

"What's up?" I ask.

Honey peers at the sky. "Rain, maybe . . ."

"No. I mean—are you *moving*?"

Honey stares at the garden. "Yes," she says. "My mother is sick. She needs me."

"Oh," I say. "I'm sorry."

"Me too."

I kneel down. *My* knees get muddy. Just like Honey's.

The next day, I lie under the sunflowers and watch
Honey plant strawberries.

Chickens doze. A bee buzzes.

"You know, there might be wasps where you're
moving to," I warn her. "Or tornadoes."

Honey turns to me and smiles. "I'll miss you too," she says.

I touch a strawberry leaf, dark and glossy. It trembles.

We walk to the porch for a cool glass of water.

"When will the berries be ready?" I ask.

"Next summer," says Honey.

"But then . . . you won't be here to eat them."

Honey takes off her gloves. "Nope," she says. "But someone will."

"That's not fair," I say. "It's *your* garden."

"This garden isn't really mine," says Honey. "It belongs to everyone."

"But you did all the work," I say.

Honey shakes her head. "I didn't plant the grapes. I only ate them."

"Then who did?"

Honey shrugs. "No way to know. But that's just fine. The new folks will enjoy these strawberries, the way I enjoyed the grapes. And if *they* add something, the garden will keep going . . . maybe forever."

The next day, I ask to plant a tree. Apples are my favorite.

We dig and dig. I get blisters.

But when we're finished, Honey says the tree will last a long, long time. "Like a person," she tells me, "but with flowers."

Honey and Laurel's tree

I make a sign. So people will know.

And then . . .

After that, Mom has to remember to buy eggs at the store.

They aren't speckled at all.

And nobody eats in the garden.

But one day, there are new people at Honey's.

Lots of people.

Little people!

They don't seem to know anything about gardens.

So I help.

Each day, I slip over the fence
to check on things.

I weed the rows.

I say hi to my tree.

Sometimes . . .

I sing to the kale.

And you know what?

When the world is very quiet, if I close my eyes . . .

I can almost hear it

singing back.